The Junkyard Dragon

R

For Hannah,
'cos you are never too old for a story about dragons!
And to Zac and Billy, who might just be reading this over your shoulder...
With love from 'Auntie Beth'   BW

For Francesca,
my beautiful baby girl   RJ

The Junkyard Dragon

Beth Webb

Illustrated by Russell Julian

LION
CHILDREN'S

Daisy wanted a dragon for her birthday.

A jaw-snapping, scale-rattling, wing-beating,
fire-breathing, real live DRAGON!

And it had to be T H I S big!

Daisy's brother Mike took her to the pet shop.
They saw slow worms and salamanders, lizards and
snakes which all looked a bit like little dragons.

But their scales didn't RATTLE!
And their jaws didn't SNAP!
They didn't breathe FIRE!
And they had no wings to FLAP!

So Daisy said 'No thank you,' to the pet shop lady
and to Mike. Then she went home feeling a little
bit sad.

For tea, Mum made Daisy's sausage, mash and greens into a dragon flying through the clouds. Daisy called him 'Fred' and ate him all up.

Then she went upstairs and read her favourite book, which was all about dragons.

Next day, Daisy's Uncle Max asked her what she wanted for her birthday. She said, 'A jaw-snapping, scale-rattling, wing-beating, fire-breathing, real live DRAGON...
And I'd like him to be T H I S big! (Please.)'
So Uncle Max took Daisy to the zoo.
They saw caiman and crocodiles and even a Komodo dragon.
Their jaws went SNAP! and their scales went RATTLE!
and they looked very fierce.

Daisy liked being 'nice' scared.

'I don't expect the zoo man will let us take one home,' said Uncle Max.

'That's all right,' Daisy said. 'MY dragon has to breathe FIRE and have wings that FLAP!

'But thank you for taking me to the zoo.'

She gave Uncle Max a big hug and went home feeling a little bit sad.

Next morning, Mum asked Daisy what she wanted for her birthday. She said, 'I'd like a jaw-snapping, scale-rattling, wing-flapping, fire-breathing, real live DRAGON... and I'd like him to be

T H I S big! (Please).'

So Mum took Daisy to the museum.
They looked at the model dinosaurs.
They all had scales that rattled and
jaws that snapped. And the
pterodactyls had wings that FLAPPED!
... And they were all REALLY BIG!

To cheer he
paints. Toge

'Why aren't they breathing fire?' Daisy whispered.

'They're only models,' Mum said. 'And I don't think dinosaurs breathed fire... They aren't <u>quite</u> dragons are they, love?'

'I know,' Daisy sniffed. 'A dragon is what I really, really want!'

Mum gave her a hug and they went home.

Next mor
It was th
were har

He was growling and groaning and roaring and rattling
and snapping loudly enough to keep the whole town awake!
He had enormous wings that swung this way and that,
flapping in the night.

But best of all, he was breathing REAL fire!

'I'll call him Fire-dinand!' whispered Daisy.

Just then, Mum and Mike and Uncle Max came in to kiss
Daisy goodnight.
   'What a noise!' Mum said. 'The people in the junkyard
must be working late.'

'Don't be silly, Mum,' said Daisy. 'It's a real live dragon!
It's _my_ real live dragon!'
   'And he has jaws that go **SNAP!**' said Mike.
   'And he has scales that **RATTLE!**' said Uncle Max.
   'And wings that go **FLAP!**' said Mum.
   '... And he's breathing **REAL fire!**' squealed Daisy.

'But I think he's too big to bring indoors, don't you?' asked Mum.

'By the look of him,' said Mike, 'I'd say he was a very <u>wild</u> dragon who will want to fly away by morning.'

'I expect he's just come to say Happy Birthday,' said Uncle Max.

Daisy pressed her nose against the window pane and watched Fire-dinand for a long time. Then she snuggled down and dreamed of flying on his back.

When Daisy woke in the morning, there was an ENORMOUS parcel at the end of her bed. She pulled all the paper off and there was the most splendiferous dragon imaginable.

'MUM! Mum! Fire-dinand has left me a dragon for my birthday and it's made out of bits and pieces, just like he was!'

'Is it big enough, do you think dear?' yawned Mum.

Daisy thought for a moment. 'Well, it's only T H I S big, but I think that's about the right size for me, don't you? I'll call him "Softie" 'cause he's cute and cuddly and comfy.' And Daisy jumped onto Softie's squashy back and laughed.

She was very happy.

Text copyright © 2007 Beth Webb
Illustrations copyright © 2007 Russell Julian
This edition copyright © 2007 Lion Hudson

The moral rights of the author and illustrator
have been asserted

A Lion Children's Book
an imprint of
Lion Hudson plc
Mayfield House, 256 Banbury Road,
Oxford OX2 7DH, England
www.lionhudson.com
ISBN-13: 978 0 7459 6008 1
First edition 2006
1 3 5 7 9 10 8 6 4 2 0

A catalogue record for this book is available
from the British Library

Typeset in 16/24 Comic Sans
Printed and bound in China